I0741783

Oh Hell, Donna!

Writer and Artist
Rowyn Golde

Print Formatting
Robert Silver

Everything Else
Rowyn Golde

www.RowynGolde.com

ISBN 978-0-692-83530-2

TEAM
MANTICORE

Oh Hell, Donna!
Volume 2:
In Between
by Rowyn Golde

This second volume is dedicated to Mike and Laura Allred.

Their colaboration both on and off the page taught me so much about comics
as an art form, and the beauty of finding your perfect partner.
No matter how dark the story gets, a splash of color can bring the whole thing to life.

Thank you,
Rowyn

The same old songs, at last they ate my heart. They wound it down until it fell apart... And all I wanted was a brand new start... Where did you go? Where are you now? Hey, can I follow? I don't know how... I never told you how I felt. On shattered knees I often knelt, but I'm trying not to break and melt. I miss you. I love you... The same old songs... Same old songs...
1987
At last, they ate my heart
I've tried this every full moon for years. You gonna work this time? No? Then time to break out the big guns.
1998
Present Day
EVIDENCE
Now time for some real rock and roll!

1

2

So then the Nazi in the ski mask got his head knocked off by the tree-demon, who turned out to be a hot chick named Donna.
If Todd met a hot chick, why didn't he introduce us yet?
I would never introduce a hot chick to any of us.
Good point.
Of course, we DID see two of his other new friends. No tree-demon, but they seem nice.
Yeah!
That would be a great idea for a campaign!
Guys, Todd said this really happened though.
So, he's crazy.
DUDE. Todd is my best friend. Don't say that shit. I KNOW he's crazy.
Sooo... How hot do you think the tree-demon-girl is?

Donna, you need rest. You were Up far too long.
I know!
I know... I just... I don't want to waste any time while he's still here. You know?
Todd is healing. Asleep. As you should be.
I wanna be here when he wakes up...

4

He's gonna be okay, right?
Of course. Look! He's waking up.
Did... Am I dead?
No. Came pretty close though.
How long was I out?
A few hours. I felt so bad. I couldn't heal you.
Why not?
I can only do outright wounds, like cuts and sometimes burns. Plus, you're magic.
Huh. Good to know.
...Fuck?
CALENDAR
I know, right??

Believe me, I'm grateful for everything you've done, but why bring me here?
I don't know... It looked like we screwed up all the evil plans involved, but I didn't want you half-dead and pulled into a plan B.
And... I wanted a break. With you. I figured down here, you could practice your power.
Donna, I like you. A lot. But I've got a life, you know? What about finding a job again? What about my friends? My parents?
We left a note!
New girlfriend took son to Underworld.
Be back later.
Milk in fridge.
-Donna
Well, at least they left a note...?

I know Tiger left, but I'm curious now. Was he born like that?
I guess. I mean, he didn't die. He was made here, like the guys with horns.
Sometimes they come out a little fucked up though, like Zippy.
What about you? If that isn't a rude question.
It isn't. I just don't remember the details. I know my friends and I died... I'm sure someone else could say more.
I forgot random things too. Like duct tape! I must've known about it at some point, but I forgot it. I don't know why.
I hope it's not too sad a thing.
Hopefully not.

So, okay. For those of us still alive, does magic change a person's body?
Sure. Just like I can change my body fat and skin around... and even kind of my hair...
Really alive magic users, rather than dead magic people sometimes change without choice.
Cause, I've been wearing the same two shirts for like a week as nothing fits anymore.
Oooo...
Yeah. It's because you've done magic, I guess.
I said a word once. Twice. It was the same phrase each time, and only because you had said it. I'm using your magic?
Other way around. The words did something because you already had the power.
It's that orb, isn't it?
Rage talks about an orb... Maybe?

He's right though. Todd really can't stay.
I know. I just didn't know what else to...
She's been up too long.
Will she be okay?
Let's all have a rest. Then she can say goodbye before the powers kick you back up, yeah?

9

Dysmorphia
Uhh... You okay?
AAAHHHH
Dysmorphia
Dysmorphia
Dys
Dysmorphia
Dysmorphia
Dysm
Gasp!
You okay?
...Yeah.
Could've slept with me, you know.
Maybe after another date.

Your friend here will be sucked up in a few hours.
Will I be able to see him again?
This is, I suppose, a special circumstance. It will be up to the Powers though.
I have things I should be doing in the meantime anyway. Find a job, an apartment... But I do want to see you again.
Soon.
And have another date?
Yeah.

Hey... I mean... About what I can do. My powers? I do move my body parts around a little. Like, if I wanna look better in a dress. I know Tiger says it's like lying but—
Plenty of people wear makeup, get surgery, all kinds of things. If you change yourself to look more like how you feel, or what you like, why would that be a problem? The issue comes in if you've been doing it for someone else.
Besides, doesn't the whole turning-into-a-cat thing make him a hypocrite then?
Fair enough.
Oh my shit! Just fuck already.
See Todd? Here is an example of someone who, like me, was alive before, but he didn't get the same treatment.
No no. This one is being punished because he's a giant asshole.
Kids these days. At least I'm consistent. The assholes you go for tend to be a bit more completely full of shit. Like Tiger? Dude's got more than two faces, if you catch my drift.
At least you know where I stand.
Stand?
Shut up.

12

Anyway, what made you think this guy would be safer down here?
We can keep a better eye on things from here. That's all.
And what about his life, like he was saying? Time still goes on up there, doesn't it?
You know what? It's worth it. I feel right when I'm with you, Donna.
We've barely had time to get to know each other...
We'll find time. Somehow.
You know, we all got origin stories. Even me.
Bored, that we weren't talking about you for five seconds?
I'll forgive it.
So... who were you? Do you remember?
How could I forget?

Can't stop thinking about
Frustrated
session
Trapped
To dust to dust
a crush
nhuman nies plo confronting s own spread Fro stay photo sep
Unloved killer isolate
Desire motivated cuttin
tribal mystery cry
growing in
mind abd believe
against ign believe on
deceptive

"Do you still love me, Phoebe?"
Yes.
Really? That's interesting. Do you know what I found?
Oh God...
chains?
Who is this? Phoebe?
My, my...
Husband.
Morgan, you don't understand. He and I were awful together...
You've been using me to cheat on your husband!
I don't take well to being the other man, you know.
fucking photo
Paper cut!
Tell me, do you still love me?
Yes. I'm sorry... I do! Yes.
How about now?
What is—
AAAAAAAH

You may as well take off the ring.
I'm afraid you're a widow now, Phoebe!
So tell me, Darling... Do you still love me?
No.
But...
I took away your guilt! I gave you a free ticket out of that marriage! He's artwork now. Can't you see that? You ungrateful, low class...
No! PLEASE—
Ding Dong
Ding Dong
Uh... Just a minute. Hold on please!

I must've killed a hundred people. They put me in an asylum! My own sister killed me, and she probably had no idea who I even was. I can't even say I regret it.
And now he's a dickless chandelier.
Of course, there's the not giving a shit about my corpse part...
What?
Yeah. I'm still where I died, under the asylum, trying to escape. Found me and left me literally to rot.
In any case, I do understand why I'm here. That doesn't mean I wouldn't snap your neck if I could...
Actually, I'd let you have a look at my journals.
Oh. They were just to die for.

Whatchoo lookin'at, Bei? Do you Know what to do with the blood?
Actually, yes.
I don't know if I'd lose my powers, but right now I'm more dead than alive.
Is that why only certain people can hear you talk?
Those with magic, or those close to death. Yep.
Will this help you speak out loud?
With other ingredients, yes.
I could join the rank of the truly undead, which would be preferable to this limbo.
Of course, if I screw it up, I'll be really dead-dead.
That would also be okay by me.

You aren't like Donna and Rage.
No. Donna died and then came half way back. Rage was given magic by my father, and then died. I died long before. Fair and square. I was never meant to be brought back.
Your dad never seemed quite right with it either.
My father made a selfish pact, not knowing what it would mean...
...for me.
However, I know he did it out of love. So, I'm not angry. I do love him and I do understand, but I don't want to go on like this.
I want to talk to Ed...
Then, we'll help you! What do you need?

19

You need bodies, don't you?
Let's see what I can do.
AAAAAAAAH
She's arachnophobic.
oh.
Is that better?
Yes.
We're gonna need more blood.

I think I'm getting pulled up.
I'll miss you. WAIT! Before you go... Here.
I see no difference.
Really? Wait. Are you making fun of me?
Not at all.
You are always beautiful. No matter what. Remember that, okay? And let's figure out how to contact each other without the—
Sigh
Beautiful.

Let's leave.
Where are we going?
I don't care.
Wait! Aren't you the girl Queenie had—
YAAH
Better... But we still need more blood...

-belmor... ARISE!
Who the fuck are you?

I already miss Todd.
What do we do now?
Well, we don't know what "the army" is doing, or if it even exists. We don't know where the guy who wanted to kill Todd is... BUT we do know the Queenie Vampire is dead, and we DO know that we can help Bei... maybe. So let's do that.
What stuff you say you need?
Some from the Underworld, and some from Up.
The vampire's blood (We already have)... The power from the orb, and the one who cursed me...
My father has to perform the ritual releasing me.
What does "releasing" mean here?
Anything other than this.
Well, first things first then. Let's go get that orb back. He had it at the castle, right?

Reduced to a Kneecap...
I feel a lot of blood. Is it alive? I can't tell.
Oh.
Poke.
SPLOOSH

This is getting ridiculous.
Awesome!
Let's go to my apartment, assuming I haven't been kicked out.
YAAAAAHHHHHHHHHHHHH

In my defense, I was trying to get Donna. ...Not you.
Our bassist? If you wanted Donna, why'd you use my microphone?
Huh. I guess she took over when you died.
Good for Donna.
WAIT. If you're summoning her- HOLY SHIT she's DEAD?
Well, yeah. Your whole band is. Even your manager.
We got a MANAG-
Look, I gotta figure out what went wrong here. Either help me, or get lost.
Humph! Fine. I'm going. I'm not gonna help you do whatever kinky shit you're tryin' to do to my friend. You're on your own... Try anything funny and she'd just kick your ass anyway... So. Fine.

Rage, can you sense where the orb is?
Ye. And he's right next to it.
Then lead the way!
He feels angry.
He's about to get more so, I'd imagine.
YOU! I know she was one of yours!
Uh-huzzuh-wazzit?
What are you doing here now?? Come to shove in my face the fact that you all survived? The fact that your people took EVERY SINGLE THING from me???
Hokay. Hold on here... What are you talking about?
Don't act like you don't know. After you killed the only person who could put The Army together... After that bitch killed what was left of my brother AND got away? NO.

Look, we just need to borrow that orb for a friend. She's cursed, and we think that orb—
HA. If I can't get what I want, NO ONE can, ever again.

HA! Now you'll never be able to do... Whatever-the-fuck you were gonna do.
Oh, and you might wanna check on your little living boy-toy. He'll be feeling the pain of this...
If he survives at all...
Heartburn?
AAAHH!
Are you okay? I heard a-OH MY GOD let's get you to a hospital!

What happened to him?
Oh, you really did have feelings for him, huh? Too bad about that... No reversal.
Especially if he's dead.
What do you care if he dies? Isn't that your thing?
That isn't how it works. He could be lost—
Well what are you gonna do about it, Dysmorphia? Heal me to death?
Yes.
Ehh...
He's suffocating.
MMMM
Rage, is Todd dead?
Nope. I think he's okay. Feels weak, but okay.
We can't stay up long. Let's go back home and see what else we can do for Bei.

You okay?
I'm dead already. You can't get me sick. I'll take you to a vet... wait.
Those aren't mine...
ACK!
I can... Can I do that for people too?

My father has news. I sent him to check on Todd.
Is he okay?
Yes, but he's got a mark on him...
What kinda Mark?
I'm telling you, he just came out of the shower and there it was!
How high are you right now, son?
Lie lie lie THINK OF SOMETHING
A pipe broke. Didn't realize I'd upped the heat. I tripped and fell forward. I mean... It's a burn, right?
Ah. Yes.

Okay. We don't have the orb anymore, but maybe there's another one?
Or maybe there's some other... Oh... I don't know...
It's okay. I'm happy you tried to help me.
Yeah. It's a start. That's what it is! We'll figure it out. We will. And then we'll have more Up stuff so we can check on Todd - and oh my crap I've ruined his life.
No. No. No. Please, don't think like that. And yes, sure. We'll find my cure eventually.
I couldn't help but overhear. I may have your solutions...

The Mechanic?
He exists in the spaces between, though he was once more like your friend Todd.
He was human, you mean.
Yes.
Now, he wonders in place. But it is not my role to tell his story, and in order to get to him, you'll need a portal. I'd show you the way, but I can not leave here.
I'll give you the recipe.
Though beware. His suggestions are often more like demands, and they do not generally lead down a thornless path.

So..."recipe" rather than ritual?
Is the same. Look see?
I guess she's right. Okay. Step one.
Bei, you hold the map, okay?
And Rage lights the candle...
Okay. So we burn this signal thing over the candle...
And we call The Mechanic?
It says... Taimult.

Heard you were dating a harpy.
Oh, she's not THAT ba-
Neat.
Can I help you?
If you're The Mechanic, we're looking for the pieces and the ritual... Stuff to lift Bei's curse, but have her not, like, be a... rotting corpse or whatever.
Okay.
Okay?
Yeah.

So, what do you think of their predicament?
This is my boyfriend, by the way. Taimult. He's the one who said you were gonna show up.
How did you know then?
My old friend Brent sent a notice.
In fact, I may know a piece of your puzzle. I won't know the rest though.
Do you, Honey?
Sure. You'll still need to get to the person who did this to her, same as before. So, here's hoping that person is still around. It's like a sealant. Steps before that change though.
Smart AND handsome.
Okay yeah, but what about the rest of it? Like... before the end?

It's an easy fix. You're already done with most of the work.
How so?
You died. Once you were dead, your father brought your body back, and preserved you with another spell. The aching you have probably been feeling is your soul trying to leave you.
And this is an easy fix?
Yeah. She's already been dead and undead. Trick now is to reconnect the pieces. Your friend still has a body, even if she's mostly other stuff, whereas... Like YOUR body is actually an empty corpse somewhere on Earth, right?
I never thought about-
Right!
Right.
So, we have to nudge you into a different state, out of your body.
Will you kill me to do it?
What? No. Of course not. No need.

39

We'll need a restless spirit.
Ah yes. That would solve multiple issues.
I'm curious. What will a restless spirit do?
Ah. It's a trade. One which benefits all parties involved. Calm the spirit down, spirit moves on, you use that ...glue left over to stick yourself to one side or the other. It is that simple.
Can you find us a spirit?
I have one in mind, but I'll need your help to help her.
Who is it?
Story time!

40

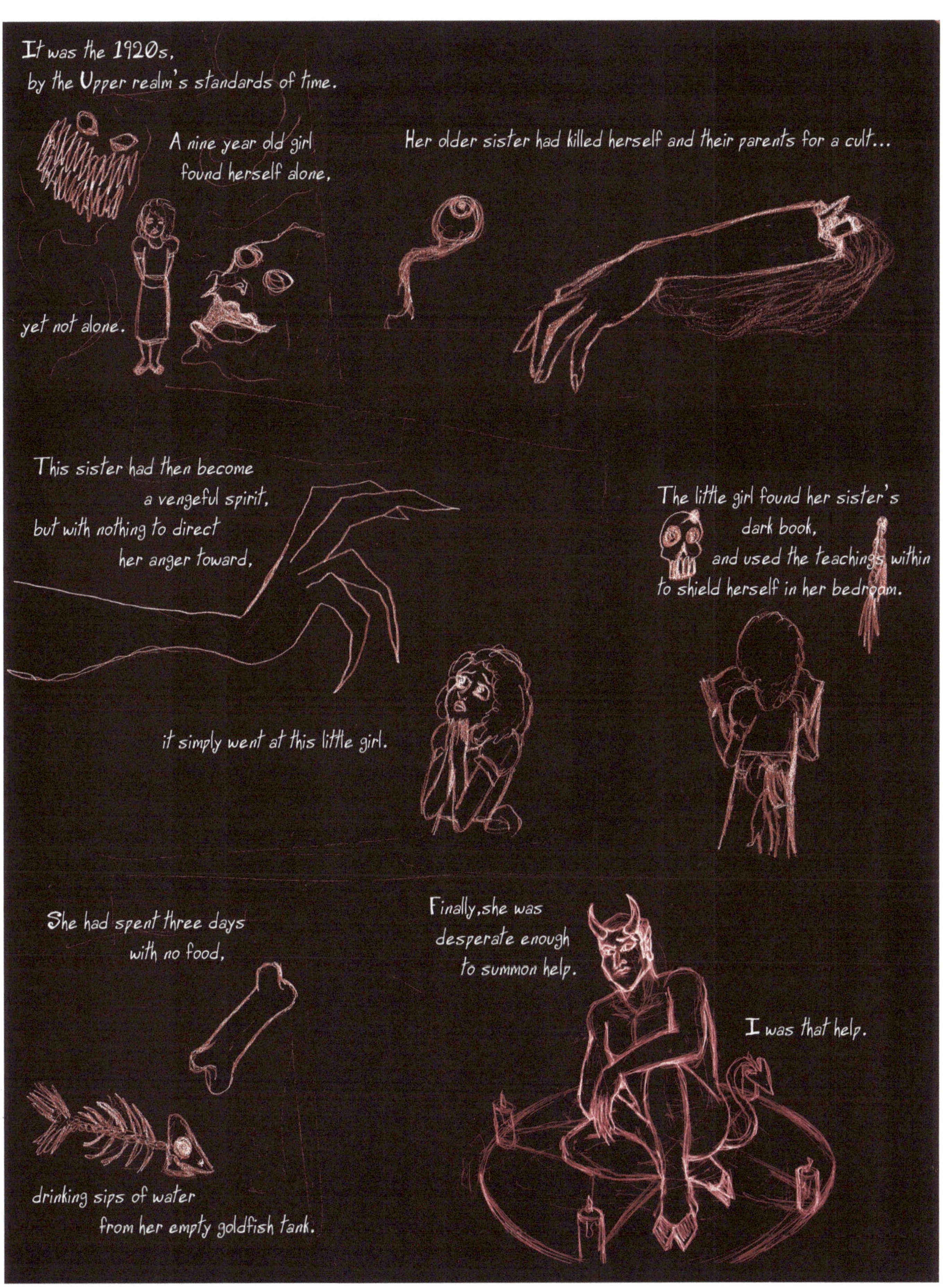

It was the 1920s,
by the Upper realm's standards of time.

A nine year old girl
found herself alone,

yet not alone.

Her older sister had killed herself and their parents for a cult...

This sister had then become
a vengeful spirit,
but with nothing to direct
her anger toward,

it simply went at this little girl.

The little girl found her sister's
dark book,
and used the teachings within
to shield herself in her bedroom.

She had spent three days
with no food,

Finally, she was
desperate enough
to summon help.

I was that help.

drinking sips of water
from her empty goldfish tank.

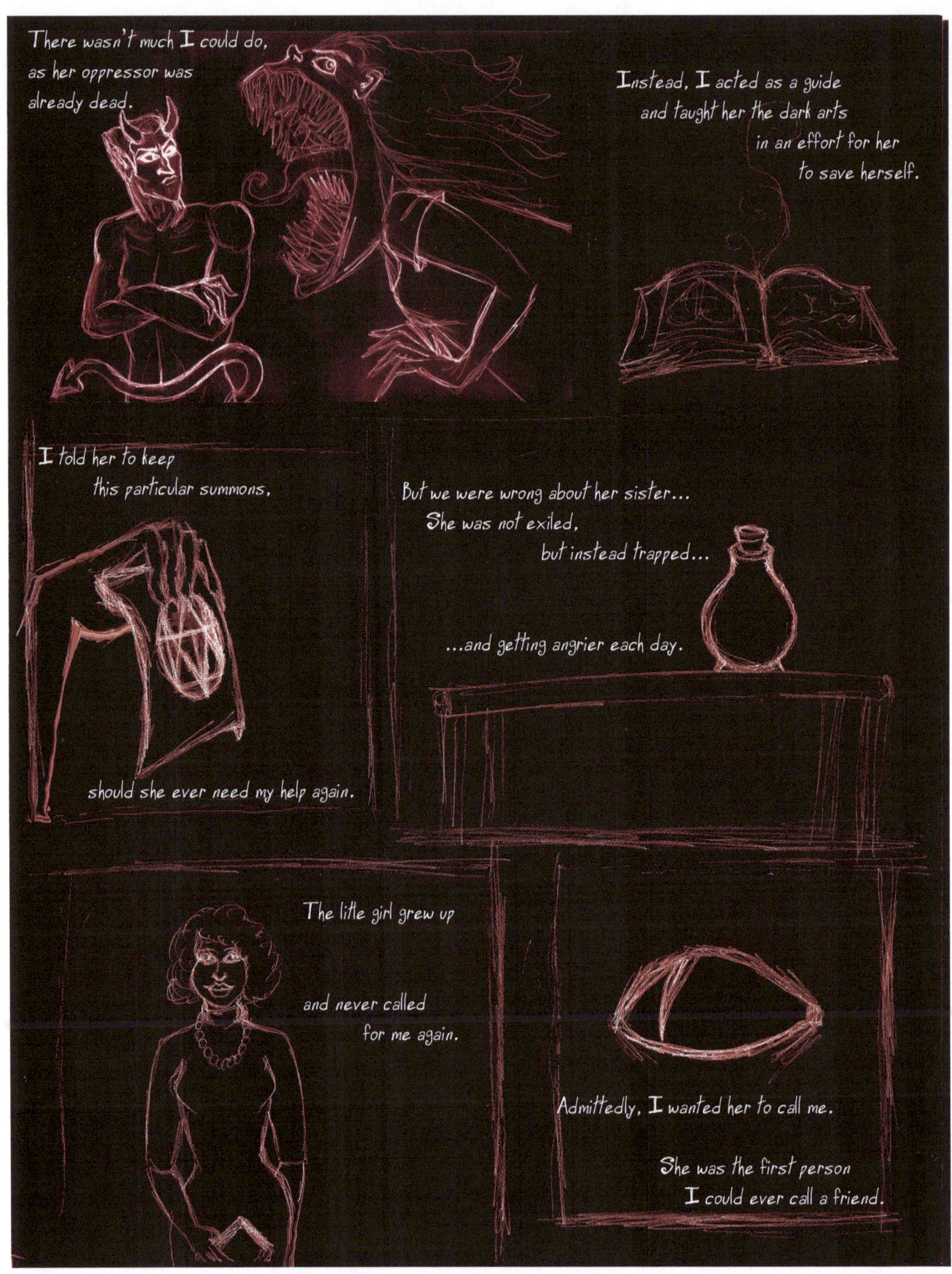

There wasn't much I could do, as her oppressor was already dead.

Instead, I acted as a guide and taught her the dark arts in an effort for her to save herself.

I told her to keep this particular summons,

But we were wrong about her sister... She was not exiled, but instead trapped...

...and getting angrier each day.

should she ever need my help again.

The little girl grew up and never called for me again.

Admittedly, I wanted her to call me.

She was the first person I could ever call a friend.

In the 1940s, she had married...
and given birth to a son.
That son grew up to be very curious...
Which proved to be his downfall.
There were suspicions as to what had happened to the boy...
Her son grew up and married sometime in the 1960s.
They had two daughters who were very close.

The eldest wanted to be a doctor.

It didn't work out.

The youngest formed a band in her teenage years, and sang with her friends.

I don't wanna BE another cog in the machine! I just gotta be ME if you get what I mean!

The son himself had been a violent man due to the ghost in his heart for all the years his daughters had been alive.

He had brutally murdered his wife years previous, and while the daughters both had suspicions, neither had proof.

The eldest turned to prostitution, seeing no other way to live
The youngest found her grandmother's old book and the folded page with my address.
She kept it in her pocket.
after the horrors her father had committed against her.
She did not know what it was for, but found herself desperate to stop her father...
and thought the page might help somehow.
Meanwhile, my old friend was only in her sixties when a heart attack did her in.
It was the 1980s then. Her son was a monster,
She died consumed by the guilt of what her son had become.
and I could only sit and watch.

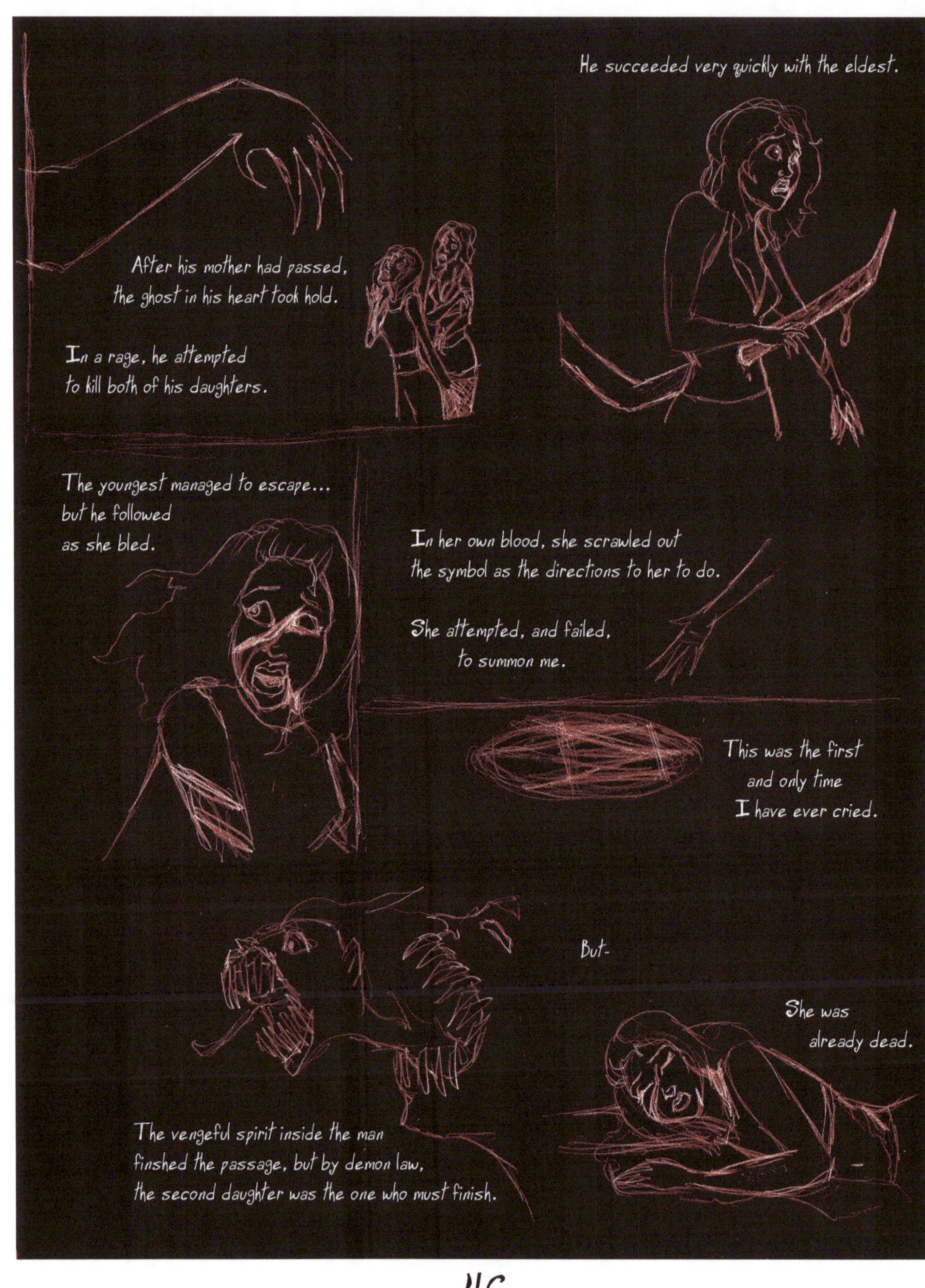

He succeeded very quickly with the eldest.

After his mother had passed,
the ghost in his heart took hold.

In a rage, he attempted
to kill both of his daughters.

The youngest managed to escape...
but he followed
as she bled.

In her own blood, she scrawled out
the symbol as the directions to her to do.

She attempted, and failed,
to summon me.

This was the first
and only time
I have ever cried.

But-

She was
already dead.

The vengeful spirit inside the man
finshed the passage, but by demon law,
the second daughter was the one who must finish.

Her sister sat by me.

I used what little power the girl had instilled within me
to drag both the vessel of their father and the spirit of
their great aunt
into the
demon world,

to be burnt up
and forgotten.

What about the other girl?

Well, I never found her spirit, but I feel her wandering about.

In fact... Things changed recently.

Changed?

She feels attached to you. Perhaps you knew her?

In any case, someone has summoned her.

So. You can find her. You can save her.

...Someone I knew?

47

48

We need a way to enhance your soul's own power. Then, your body can just move into something more useful.
You shouldn't even look any different, but you should feel better.
No more curse?
Well, you won't have the same curse, in any case. I make no guarantees.
This kind of thing always has loopholes in both directions.
In fact... See that other kettle there?
Yeah.
Pour that into your cup, add your vial o' vampire, and drink it. I had a hunch you'd need it.
Just like that?
Just like that.

Hmm. I don't feel any-
HEY I'M TALKING AND BUGS AREN'T FLYING OUT OF MY FACE.
Yay!
So, what's the downside then?
Well, you aren't quite done yet. Death for death and all that. You'll need someone else to be a corpse before time runs out. That's why you need a lost soul. Someone who is still connected to their corpse, ready to leave it...
It's timed?? Why didn't you mention that BEFORE she drank it? How much time do we have to do thing-the thing??
The ritual has been completed. I feel it. Rozzie is out there, waiting to be found. Help her. Find her...
...Rozzie?

That mean you'll stay here with me?
The moment I leave here, anyone else could summon me. As long as I stay, I'm yours. Anyone attempts to summon me, they'll just come here, like they did. So... Yes.
Sooo... How do we get back home now? And how do we find this... Rozzie?
Donna, listen to your gut. You'll be able to find your old friend in time.
Yeah. And Bei can get back to us whenever she wants. Then she can summon the rest of you... But I don't think you'll have to come back. You should be able to just get your friend and be done... Well, THEN you gotta get to the person who cursed Bei in the first place. Now get goin'!
But how do I—
POOF

Bzz-z
Bzzz
Bzzz
WELL, that's new.
I think she'll be able to help us.
Rage, if this is really our... Well my Rozzie, can you find this person?
Yazmin

They can do this without me, right?
You chose to stay here with me... You could have gone to help.
No, I can't. Demon's law. The girl I sent them after was already a botched job on my part. Missed my shot, had there been one.
Well, as long as they help Raz before the potion fades out, everyone wins.
What makes you think those kids can help her?
She knew them.
If not?
Our new friend Bei becomes attached to the upper realm.
She rots.
And I can do nothing.
I can think of something you can do...
You really are a wonderful distraction.

Wait. Why isn't it...
Why is there pain?
Are you oka-AH!
Oh my god! Let me help!
AH!
Oh no!
Stay away!

You don't remember much, but you remember your old bandmates?
Sure. I remember some good things. It's just kind of random, I guess.
Hey... It's you, right? Donna Pierce.
Um. Yes. You a fan?
Yeah! I even brought you back from the dead! See? Look at you!
Oooh no. I was like this.
What?
Yeah. We're up here for our friend, Rozzie.
So it IS because of what I did. HAH.
Do you know where she is now?
Yeah. I followed your dead friend to the hospital.

Donna, we have to go.
HEY. You can't leave. I helped you!
Thank you for your assistance!
YAAAAHHH
I'm gonna figure this out, you know. YOU'RE GONNA BE MY GIRLFRIEEEND!
How far is it, do you think?
Hopefully not much farther. I didn't realize this would happen so fast.
Will Rage know how to send Yazmin to us?
Rage can always find me. If your friend has that sort of thing with Rozzie, yes.

Hey! Get off of her!
You don't understand. Get out of the way so we can help all these people!
That woman! All I did was touch her! I'm bleeding! I'm bleeding!
I'm —
I'm okay?
Rage has sent your friend! I feel it.

Gasp!
...Yazmin? Are you-
No, don't-
Dead. Sure. But you died first, remember?
When I died, I tried to find you...
But you weren't there. You just weren't anywhere!
I'm so sorry. But I'm here! You found me! But-

-But you can't touch me! I can't control this. I'll hurt you and-
I feel different. Lighter...
Hope you don't mind. I'm taking your... something? That means you're free now.
Then let's go, Roz. Let's go home together.
"Together"... I like that.
Hey, what happened to your leg?

There. Honestly, I was expecting some Heavenly glow or something.
So now what?
What fuck just happened?
I guess we go home? Or back to the Mechanic and Taimult... And then to see my dad.
Actually, we're already here... Let's check in on Todd! I feel him... Somewhere.
He's here?
I bet we could look up that symbol. Can't you contact Donna?
No. I don't know how.
Hey guys!
Well, that was easy.

So, what is it?
I'm not sure.
My father... might know what to do with this.
Or maybe The Mechanic?
I'm glad you got your voice back!
Hee hee Me too!
Okay, I don't entirely believe all this demon shit, but there's been too many weird things to ignore now. So. Fine.
If you get to a phone...
This is my number.
555-0158 Ed
I know you're on a mission, and we'll be fine. Still, IS there a way to get in contact with each other?
Actually, my father may be able to help with that... Or The Mechanic.
You guys have a Mechanic?

61

Another possibly inappropriate question... Are you ever in danger? I mean... I know you're already dead, but can you die? Should I worry about you?
Aw. Don't worry. If we die, there's a place we go. It's just not that same place as normal.
Anyway, I'll miss you. Stay safe.
I'll be okay. I've got a job interview tomorrow, so my main goal is to at least survive until then. ...And then see you again.
Sooo if they're gonna see each other again, does that mean WE get to see each other again?
Are you asking me out on a date?
If the answer would be "yes," then yes.
The answer is yes.
Until we meet again...

We sent them off to help someone, but I realize we didn't exactly ask if she wanted help.
That is often how the demon world works.
...You're here by choice, right?
Of course. One of the reasons I couldn't help. Like I've said, if I leave, someone else could summon me. So long as I stay, I am yours.
Please don't worry. You have been so kind.
I've been summoned to do all manner of things by all kinds of people. Even as far as sleeping with someone just because I wanted to, that never happened until you. No one else I've found attractive saw me as much more than a tool.
So, you DO find me attractive? I just want to be sure I haven't accidentally been forcing you to—
Of course not! I only want you!
You are not a tool to use.

You lied to Todd. You know fully well what happens if we "die" again.
I don't want him to be scared, okay?
How ya feelin', Roz?
MUCH better. Fuck. It was like I got so filled up with everybody else's pain that I just couldn't hide my own anymore.
You two stay happy, okay? We gotta go back to... The Mechanic.
Sigh... and then to my father. Outside of a bug. In person. When was the last time I even saw him? Donna, I think I'm nervous.
I know, but we also can't tell how this stage of things will go. You were rotting away before. This one may have a side effect too. Gotta finish what we start.
That's true. I'm tired of being half way between one place and another.

Wanna play "Rattle?"

Yeah Mom, living with Ed is pretty great, actually. OH and I got the job! I'm gonna work at the museum. I'm a docent trainer
No, I'm going to be training the guides, rather than giving tours myself. ... Well, I could give YOU and Dad a tour, yeah. Haha!
Have you told her about Donna?
Huh? Oh yeah, Donna left that note for you guys, didn't she? Ha ha... Sorry about that.
...Uh... Yeah. Quite the sense of humor. Well, obviously I'm fine and that's what matters. Yeah... Yeah, I guess Donna is my girlfriend.
Oh! Right. Of course you guys wanna meet her. She's my girlfriend. I think. Okay. Well. See, it's kind of... complicated.

Gotta find something of Donna's, if I'm gonna summon her, but where?
Wait.
No living person would Know Donna better...
Cornsbrook Asylum
08-13
You wanna hear a story?

I'm a beach ball, Baby
Just WATCH me deflate—
under
your
ego's
TEN TON
WEIGHT
I'll call you Daddy
if you take me to the
MALL! Pay for it. Pay for it.
Pay for it.
I'd call you Daddy but the
DIAMOND is too small!
Pay for it.
Pay for it.
pay for it.
Pay for it.
Can you even believe it?
Well, I mean you did wind up a legend anyway, even if it was for... other reasons.
OH. Do you even know... how that went down, Peyton?

DONNA
Donna!
Donna!
Donna
Donna
Donna!
BREZIT
Glasgow Nikki.

She's yer aunt, huh? I see the resemblance.
Do you need my ID or anything?
Nah. Got enough crazies in the Madhouse. Just take 'er.
Well, it was so nice talking to a fan again!
But I gotta go. Bye bye!
WAIT! What about something of Donna's? Don't you wanna bring her back too?? Vengeance or whatever? You said you'd lead me to something of Donna's if I got you out!
Meh. Screw her. You want something of Donna's? Go to her grave, Fan-Boy.

70

71

We don't really need to go to The Mechanic though, right?
Don't you think your dad could help us talk to the boys?
Well, probably... But—
...and fix you?
I'm AFRAID, okay?
You talk to your dad all the time though.
As a bug, sure. And even then, not really. He tells me things I need to know. That's not the same as being a father.
I don't... I don't want to see him.
I'm so worried though. I mean, are you okay? Is this good enough now?
Actually, I'm in an incredible amount of pain these days.
Then... Let's go.

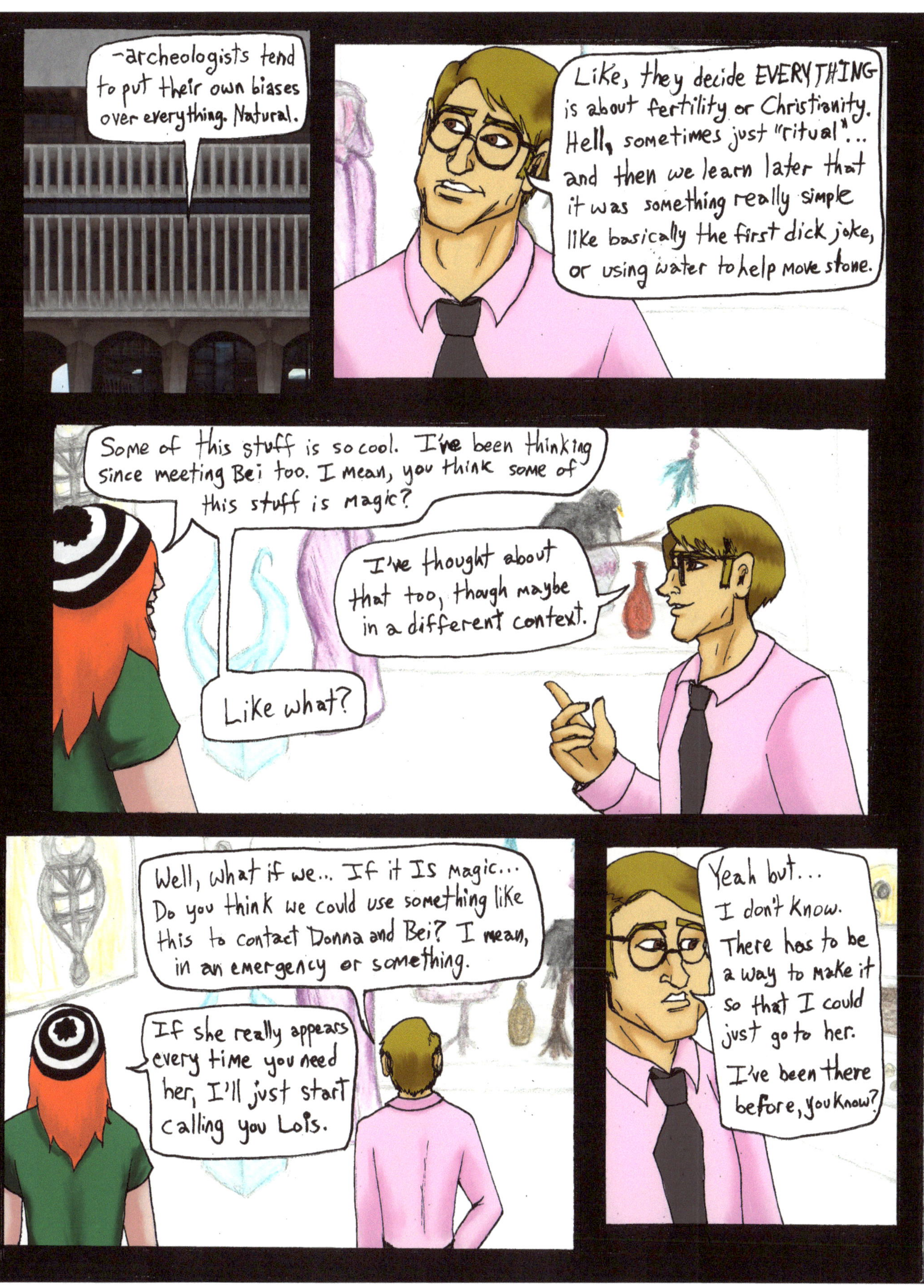

—archeologists tend to put their own biases over everything. Natural.

Like, they decide EVERYTHING is about fertility or Christianity. Hell, sometimes just "ritual"... and then we learn later that it was something really simple like basically the first dick joke, or using water to help move stone.

Some of this stuff is so cool. I've been thinking since meeting Bei too. I mean, you think some of this stuff is magic?

I've thought about that too, though maybe in a different context.

Like what?

Well, what if we... If it IS magic... Do you think we could use something like this to contact Donna and Bei? I mean, in an emergency or something.

If she really appears every time you need her, I'll just start calling you Lois.

Yeah but... I don't know. There has to be a way to make it so that I could just go to her. I've been there before, you know?

Maybe this is the way.

Dude. I don't know if I wanna join that conga line, if that's how you're gonna dance.

Yeah. You're right. I just miss her.

Yeah. I get tha- fuck is this about?

OH it's an old myth. I mean, everything here is old, but this is about the... They're like the four horsemen? Only not.

Is there an apocalypse involved?

In the sense that the total end of the world happens, no. In the sense that it's a major change... Thus the end as we know it? Yes. Absolutely.

Legend has it they will bridge the Living World with that of The Dead.

And thus, we see why messing with stuff to see our lady friends might not be so great.

They have names?

Arakep of Earth, Ohemj of Water, Sekiln of Fire, and Belnics of Air.
Dude. These guys are like THE most disconcerting Planeteers. Why? Ugh.

You ready? Let's get through the portal.
Poof
This...is not where my father is.
Must be interference from Sedona...
Then... How do we get there?
Zzzzzz

AH!
You found the place. I was worried it had been too long.
Sooo... You're the man from the bugs?
That is correct. I'm also the man who saved your lover-boy.
When? The time I sent roaches to get him from an evil man's clutches? The time Donna found him in time to rip him from a sand pit?? Or the time she dragged him to the Underworld to heal in peace??? WHEN? When were you even remotely helpful? OR DO YOU MEAN WHEN HE GOT KIDNAPPED WHILE ON YOUR WATCH? Do you mean THAT ONE?
I mean right now. I've seen it. I've seen that key in your hand.
This? You know what this is then?
Obviously I do.

Nikki, nobody remembers you. When you got that thing on your face, you look fine... But take it off... and you're a freakshow!
You don't know that! You haven't even see me.
Look at me!
Ugh...
TELL ME I'M PRETTY!
What? No. Nikki, nobody wants you.
Tell me I'm pretty.
...No.
JESUS.
Smash

Nobody wants me?
That Peyton boy wanted me...
Well, he wanted Donna, but since that's impossible, he'll take me.
Yeah! That's right! I have a fan!
Time for a come-back tour.

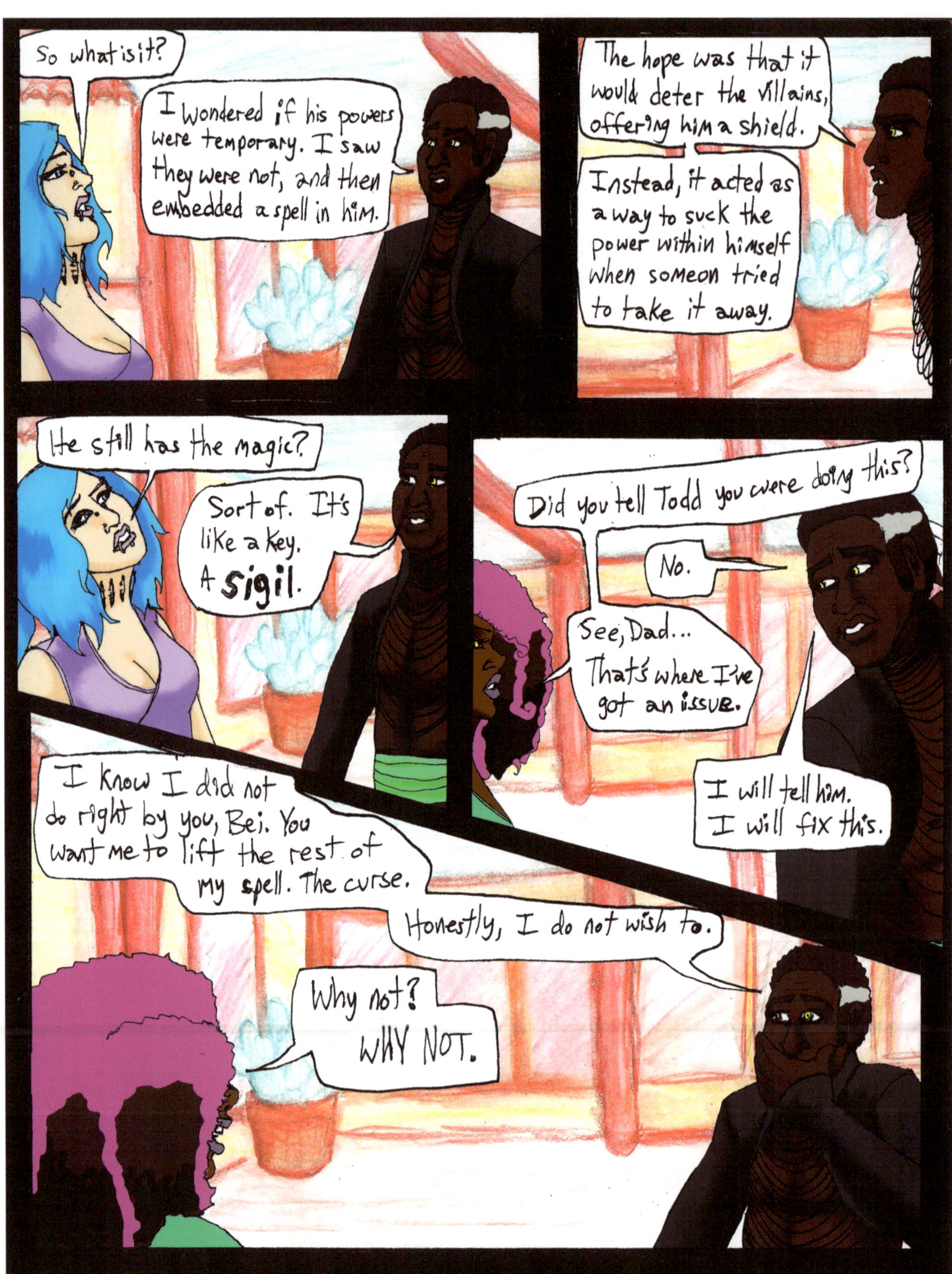

So what is it?
I wondered if his powers were temporary. I saw they were not, and then embedded a spell in him.
The hope was that it would deter the villains, offering him a shield.
Instead, it acted as a way to suck the power within himself when someon tried to take it away.
He still has the magic?
Sort of. It's like a key. A sigil.
Did you tell Todd you were doing this?
No.
See, Dad... That's where I've got an issue.
I will tell him. I will fix this.
I know I did not do right by you, Bei. You want me to lift the rest of my spell. The curse.
Honestly, I do not wish to.
Why not? WHY NOT.

I worry. Your mother has been gone a long time. My sister too. When the... sickness tried to pry you away, I panicked. I know.
And look how far you've come without me! You've got your voice back! But... I worry that if I lift this, you'll never need me again.
I barely see the real you as it is. I've spent my afterlife trapped and silent. Please. Let me go. Let me choose to come back.
I shall... think... about it.
THINK about it?? Look, we came a long way. And this is your DAUGHTER. What are you doing?

Cemetery. This is it. This is where Donna is.
Don't worry, Baby. Peyton's coming for ya!
You must get to Donna's cemetary. Something is terribly wrong!
I don't believe you! This is some kind of distraction or—
HERE! You are free.

Now take Donna
to her own corpse.

Her spirit will bond Permanently with mine!
Oh fuck. Oh FUCK that's... THAT'S-
STOP!
I can still do that?
AAAAAAAAAAAHHH

Wait. Was he doing a binding spell?
Doesn't matter right now.
I remember. I remember everything.

MRROWW
BOndEd forEVer.

Is she okay?
Remembers what?
I don't know. She just said she "remembers everything" and then stopped talking.
Oh. ... Can we find Bobby? He might help.
Yeah. I think it's high time we got the band back together.

You rang?

Ah, man. It's been a while. What's up?
Oh. You finally remember what happened, huh?
Is it that obvious?
Oof. I don't feel so good.
Let's get you some rest.

Huh. That's new.
Dysmorphia
Dysmorphia
Dysmorphia
Dysmorphia
Dysmorphia
I can't stop it!
OH FU-
...Do demons even dream?

Still having nightmares?
Nightmares? What's that about?
sigh I don't know. There was this vampire... organ-lady.
I think... she got into my head. And that was after I may or may not have sort of killed a guy? And the sky... turned red, and then I stayed up WAY too long and then I did it AGAIN because I'm a freaking moron and I just wanted to make sure he was okay because it's MY fault now if he's not, but I DID save him from getting killed to begin with and...
Yeah. Same.

Now I'm "Dysmorphia" in my dreams. I melt and I can't control anything... I mean, that probably means something. Maybe.
Yeah.
I think having Todd be in danger really screwed me up.
Besides, I'm this dead-freak, and he's...
He's not.
Yeah.
Hopefully when he dies, he'll just be normal.
I don't want him to be like this. Ever.
Yeah, but if he is, you'll take care of him.
Of course!

Relationships are rough to begin with.
One of you bein' dead doesn't make it any easier.
Speaking of which, whatever happened to your fiancé?
It took a long time for her to find someone else after I died. I'm glad she finally did.
Do you ever see her?
Of course not. I love her. It would be a cruel thing to do.
Oh. Yeah. I guess that would be, yeah.

So this is your signal now?
I guess so. And this one is for Donna.
And a bug gave this to you without any real explanation of how to use them?
It was Bei's dad, and... Yes. He said there's a book or something. Yeah. There's a book.
OH GOOD that isn't totally vague or anything...
Meh. Well, you gotta get to work. I've got a feeling this book wouldn't be in the library, so maybe I'll meet you at the museum? Yeah?
Of course, if I find it, I won't be able to touch it. WELL maybe I'll have a title to look up online or something
It's as good a plan as any.

So, let's talk about it. I literally just got done telling Rozzie about my leg, so fill her in on the rest.
Honestly, I'm pretty curious myself.
Well, when Bobby, Yazmin, and I were alive, we were squatting in this old used-to-be-an-apartment with our manager.
...My shitty boyfriend at the time.
In retrospect, I'm glad I forgot while I was becoming a stronger person. Now I can really pick through it. You know, I let Tiger get away with a lot before, but nothing like I let John do. Even before it—
...But I'm getting ahead of myself.
Hold on. See, we got snowed in...

Donna's Story!

Day...what? How many days have we been hangin' out in this RIGHTFULLY condemned building, huh? Hmm?
Nah. Jon just wanted to know what it was like to be poor and bored.
We don't need this shit anymore, Yaz. Jon ain't punk. He's gonna get us all killed.
We had to squat somewhere, Bobby. Beggars can't be choosers, right?
No, but he's our manager. He's gotten us all the good gigs - Now keep your voice down. He's gonna be done shitting any minute. The music on your crap box isn't loud enough to keep drowing out your bitching. So, what's really up? What's your real problem with Jon?
sigh...
You know he gave Donna that bruise, right?
She hasn't said so, but it's obvious.
TOO LOW

Has he hurt you?
Yeah, but he always says he's sorry an—
We'll talk later, but I'm never leaving you alone with him again.
...And Bobby might kill him.
But the band—
Doesn't matter as much as your safety.
Besides, we were doing just fine without a manager before.
You guys gonna jam or what? I play a mean keyboard, by the way. Could be manager AND keyboard...ist. Yeah!

Well, we're officially out of food. Been too long.
No heat, no electric, we don't have a phone... And now the water pipe is frozen too. We started with nothing, and now we have even less.
We gotta get out.
We're still snowed in. Even worse now. I don't—
So? We have to find a way. We do.
Oh shit. Is this the only floor we can see out of? We're like the fifth floor though!
Right.

Nah nah nah that can't be right. Hold on.
EXIT
Oh come on.
I've been to every floor...
Everything is frozen and dark and...
We're gonna die in here.

She'll just slide down the ice.
INTO TRAFFIC.
What traffic? Town's dead.
We're all gonna be dead...
I wanna go. I want to try.
Just be sure to close the window really fast after I go. Don't let too much cold in.
Are you sure?
Of course she is!
Yeah!
Do we have a rope or something?
... Like Donna said, we gotta keep that window closed so we don't freeze to death.
What about Donna freezing?
Take this. Might be useful if you find a decent dumpster to dive... And be careful.

Donna, Sweetie... This is a suicide mission. Don't do this.
It'll be okay. I was a girl scout!
That's true. It's how we met.
Nooooo confidence from that one for me.
She goes, she might have more of a chance surviving this than we do.
Okay. Steady... Here I go...
krish

Well, that didn't sound painful, at least...
Huh?
I fell into a car?
Click
Can't even see where I came from. Just snow. Looks dark through that hole...
gasp AAAHH huhu!

Ah guh
Wait.
I must have passed out, right? It's night... I should just stay here until morning.
It's like an igloo. ...With a frozen dead person.

Good morning, Slim Chance For Survival!
Pizza Knight
What hurts?
OH BAJEEZUS has that been all night?

Where are those water jugs from our last gig?
I have them. Locked away, safe and sound. Don't want to be wasting any in a time like this.
Well, can I have one?
Depends what you offer me.
What the fuck?
Oh come on, I'm just joking. Kidding around? It's a tense time, guys. HA. Relax.
It's... Mostly empty.

ACK.
Come on, Leg! I fixed you up, didn't I?
Grunt
My leg...
Why didn't I..
FWUMP

107

Pizza Knight?
I hope you don't mind. You were in our dumpster. My husband got you in through the window. I bandaged you up. Do you remember us?
Yeah. You guys let me help around for tips.
We could have just hired you, you know. But you're a musician, right? Where's your band?
Oh god. They're trapped. They're in that building and I...
Lay down, Honey. Take it easy. You were out a good day. Almost frost-bitten. If you can tell me where they are, we can call for help when the phones are back.

I... I can't think. Everything is cold.
Here. Eat.
My friends need help.
We still can't call for emergency services. Phone is still dead, and we're officially snowed in. BUT once the storm gets a little lighter, I'll go out and find someone. We'll help you, Donna. I promise.
Yeah.
Okay.

We need food. I can't go another day.
I'm so sleepy...
We'll make a fire and eat the snake.
You are NOT eating Edith.

Is the phone back?
No. But the weather is lighter.
I'm gonna dig out the truck and get help for Donna.
I have to get back to my friends. It's been like four days... More? I can't even keep track anymore.
If you wait, my husband can drop you right off —
Oh.

Ah. Okay. That didn't last long. We're gonna need more meat.
Meat? What about fucking WATER? What did you DO with it? You stupid piece of shit! Com'on, Man! I'm tired of this! You never belonged here. Not with US. You shoulda been the one to go out there and fucking die out in the cold while the rest of us—
Hterk
YAA!

Okay guys, I'm bac-

Bobby...
Gasp
...Donna?
Yazmin?
Donna. You have to leave. You shouldn't have come back...
Where is Jon?

Donna! You're back! Just in time.
Are you hungry? We're out of Edith, and Bobby isn't gonna still be good, but see... I figured that out.
I've been keeping Yazmin alive here by simply feeding herself to... herself. And me.
Clever, right? See, you know how to pick a clever man, Donna.
This way, she'll stay fresh, and you and I can survive.

116

YAZMIN! I'll get you out.
I just need to find something sharp for the tape...
No. Just... Please kill me? PLEASE. I don't want this. ...to live like this. I want to be with Rozzie. I want Edith back.
But...
He ate Edith, killed Bobby, and ate my leg. Doesn't matter now. You're here. Please. If you get me to a hospital, they'll stitch me up and I won't have the courage to do it. Kill me!
Quick! I hear people coming. Kill me bef— CRACK

We're goin' in.
BASH
DROP YOUR WEAPON
You don't understand—

BAM
BLAM
BAM

I don't blame them.
What else could they
have possibly thought?

119

Sniff
Oh God. Yazmin! I killed you! I'm so sorry.
Believe me, Honey, it was a good thing.
Suicide?
You do what you have to do to survive, and you do the kindest things you can for others with the tools given to you.
It's all we got.

Off to work! GOD it feels great to say that.
And you like it there, right?
OH yeah. The museum is great! It's got everything! You should come by and see the new exhibit.
Oooh, new exhibit, you say. Is it sexy?
NEW!
In this place, Brother Sal says they have something we can use...
Who the fuck is Brother Sal?
The guy who's gonna get this show back on track.

Coming here made all my clothes vanish?
Huh. Not a bad side effect.

Wanna unwrap
your present?